What do the grow... Sean the actor

"Utterly charming, full of facts and a great career guide."
Tony Boullemier, author of The Little Book of Monarchs.

"An informative and fun way to introduce your children to the world of living."
Gordon Buchanan, wildlife filmmaker
(BBC Springwatch, Autumnwatch, The Polar Bear Family and Me).

"Really detailed and informative books, which contain exactly the questions that intelligent children ask, and adults are often unable to answer. There is fun, humour and a wonderful sense of place too."
Dr Ken Greig, Rector, Hutchesons' Grammar School.

"As an educator in the US there is more and more stress placed upon children being able to access non-fiction writing. Within her books, Mairi McLellan has done something many children's authors are unable to do: she has created non-fiction books that are compelling and highly readable. May all of children's non-fiction literature begin to engage students as McLellan's books do. If this is a new trend in children's books, teachers across the US would be so grateful."
Marlene Moyer, 5th & 6th Grade teacher, Nevada, USA.

"What a refreshing an innovative way of introducing children to career possibilities in later life. A delightful series of books which gently guides younger children through the adult world of work. The accompanying photos of the main characters bring the lives of Joe the Fisherman, Fiona the Doctor and Papa the stockfarmer to life."
Louise Webster, broadcaster.

Matador
9 Priory Business Park
Kibworth Beauchamp
Leicestershire LE8 0RX, UK
Tel: (+44) 116 279 2299
Fax: (+44) 116 279 2277
Email: books@troubador.co.uk
Web: www.troubador.co.uk/matador

ISBN: 978 1783062 003

British Library Cataloguing in Publication Data.
A catalogue record for this book is available from the British Library.

Matador is an imprint of Troubador Publishing Ltd

www.kidseducationalbooks.com

What do the grown-ups do?

Sean the actor

Mairi McLellan

What do the grown-ups do?

Dear reader,

The **What do the grown-ups do?** series is designed to educate children about the workplace, and the world around them, in a light-hearted and interesting manner. The ideal age range is five to ten years old and feedback from the children has been fantastic.

The aim is to offer the children an insight into adult working life, to stimulate their thinking and to help motivate them to learn more about the jobs that interest them. Perhaps by introducing these concepts early, we can broaden their ideas for the future, as well as increase their awareness of the world around them. It's just a start, and at this age, although the message is serious, it is designed to be fun.

For younger children, who will be doing a combination of reading and 'being read to', this series will be reasonably challenging. I have deliberately tried not to over-simplify the books, to maintain reality, whilst keeping the tone chatty and informal.

The books can be read in any order, but they are probably best starting from the beginning. The order of the series can be found at the back of this book. Many more will be coming soon, so please check the website for updates **www.kidseducationalbooks.com.**

I hope you enjoy them.

Happy reading,

Mairi

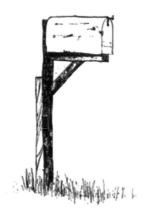

A note of thanks to my wonderful skin and blister, my fabulous sister, Fiona for her humour and fun. They say you can't choose your family but I would have chosen you. Also, to all from *Songs for Amy* - Konrad, Jim, Ultan, Alabama 3, Gavin, Kevin, Ford, Lorna, Ross, Barry, Duncan, Mari, Marc, and the rest of the gang. Lastly, and very importantly, to the lovely Sean Maguire. Great film, great times. Viva Badaneel.

Life by the sea in Badaneel

Ava, Skye and Gracie Mackenzie lived in Badaneel, a pretty little village by the sea, in the northwest Highlands of Scotland. It was the most beautiful place, surrounded by impressive mountains, where heather clad hills swept down to meet wide sandy beaches.

The snow-capped mountains around Badaneel.

The twins, Ava and Skye were six years old and Gracie had just turned five. The Mackenzie girls were all the same height and looked like triplets, with long, blondish, wind-swept hair. As sisters and best friends, they went everywhere together and shared a tiny room with two sets of bunk-beds. They shared their clothes, their toys and even their classroom at the local school.

It was winter in Badaneel and despite the very disappointing lack of snow, the girls had come up with the cunning plan of sledging down the sand dunes. Point beach offered the best dunes by far. They were massive and bright red in colour as they were made from crushed red sandstone.

Massive dunes at Point beach.

From the very top of the dunes were fabulous views over to the Outer Isles, but more importantly, a grassy ramp that was used to get extra speed on the sledge!

Gracie at the bottom of the dune.

The Mackenzie girls and their cousins had hours of entertainment on the dunes, with competitions to see who could slide the furthest. When they reached the bottom, each person would mark their name in the sand, beside the track marks of their sledge. It was normally cousin Molly who won!

Dune sledging competitions!

Molly marking the score.

Dune sledging was usually followed by playing in the sea, where jumping the waves had the predictable result of wet wellies, followed by a speedy trip home to the bath, before everyone froze! After a day in the cold fresh air, the exhausted trio would settle in front of the fire to watch television before heading off to bed, with Ava and Skye on the top bunks and Gracie down below.

Jumping the waves at Point beach.

Jobs

The girls spent a lot of time playing but they also had jobs to do. Ava, Skye and Gracie got their pocket money by working and earned one pound per hour. Their jobs included:

- Gathering logs
- Scraping the barnacles off the bottom of the dinghy
- Vacuuming the house
- Peeling vegetables
- Setting the table
- Unloading the dishwasher
- Tidying their wardrobe
- Cleaning the car
- Collecting leaves from the lawn
- And many more…

They didn't mind their jobs as it meant they could buy whatever they liked. Recently they had saved up twenty pounds each to buy fantastic new snow boots. There was no-one in the village with cosier feet than the Mackenzie girls!

Today the jobs were in the garden. The winter winds had brought down all sorts of twigs, small branches and leaves, which needed gathered up and put onto a bonfire pile.

The girls were good workers, although there was often debate about who had the rake, who had the shovel and who had to carry the basket down to the shore. If they were caught arguing for too long, or caught being lazy, then pocket money was reduced and so disputes had to get sorted out as quickly as possible!

"I've had enough now Mama," said Gracie after a mere 20 minutes. "Can I go and watch television please?"

"I hardly think so, Gracie," said Mother. "If this was a proper job you would be in trouble for lack of effort! We need two hours today in the garden to clear these leaves and branches. After that you can go and watch television or do whatever you like," she said.

Skye and Gracie gathering leaves.

Mother said that it was important to have fun in life, especially when you are young, but it was also important to understand about work because when you grow up, everyone needs to work to earn money for a house, clothes, food and so on.

Gracie smiled. She was a chancer and felt it was always worth asking, just in case work might be finished early for the day.

"I'm looking forward to getting a grown-up job," said Ava. "Then I won't get told what to do all the time!"

"Well that depends on what job you get, Ava," said Mother. "If you go to work for someone else, then they will be telling you what to do!" she said. "If you don't want someone telling you what to do, then you either need to be very good at your job, so that you don't need instructions, or you need to start up your own business, which has its own challenges," she smiled.

"How about not working at all?" said Skye laughing.

"Well you can do that too but there will be no house and no money to buy sweeties," said Mother. "The best thing to do is to work at something you enjoy so that it doesn't feel like work," she smiled.

"What jobs do the people who make television do, Mama?" asked Gracie.

"Hmmm, well there are a large amount of people involved in making television as well as a several different companies. If you want to make a film, you need a writer, actors, a director, cameramen and sound engineers, not to mention all sorts of jobs in between to handle costumes, make-up, props, music, accounts, editing and many more. Making a television program or a film involves a wide variety of different jobs, many of which are very specialized," she explained.

"Would you like to meet an actor to find out more about what they do?" asked Mother.

"Yay! That would be great! Do you know one, Mama?" asked Skye.

"Well, your auntie Yaya has just finished making a film and the main actor is a lovely man called Sean Maguire. I've met him lots of times and he's great fun. As it happens, Auntie Yaya is showing her film here in Badaneel so he will be visiting soon! I'll ask him if he could spare time to have a quick chat with you. I'm sure he won't mind at all," she said.

Sean the actor

The Badaneel café was transformed into a mini cinema where Auntie Yaya and some of the actors met with the local villagers to promote the film. Sean was expecting them as the Mackenzie girls wandered over rather nervously. "Hello," said Gracie, who was always first to introduce herself. The twins shuffled behind, not sure what to say.

"Hi girls," said Sean with a big smile. "I've heard so much about you! I'm glad you could come and join us. Your Mum told me that you want to find out what actors do. Is that right?" he asked.

He had a really friendly face and a slightly different accent from the one they were used to in Badaneel.

"Yes please," said Gracie. "We are investigating grown-up jobs and we wondered what it was like to work in film and television," she said, quite matter of factly.

"Well, I'd be delighted to help," smiled Sean. "What would you like to know?" he asked.

"Can you tell us what actors do?" asked Skye.

"Actors and actresses basically pretend to be other people for a living," said Sean. "We often have to learn how to speak in a different accent, or change our behaviour on the film-set, to make our characters seem more real. For example, sometimes we do funny dances and things that make people laugh, if it is a comedy. Other times, we have to be really serious and pretend to be angry or upset. Each character is different," he explained.

Sean pretends to be annoyed, whilst his friend pretends to dance, in the film, *Songs for Amy*.

"Is that why you sound different?" asked Gracie.

Sean laughed. "No, that's not acting, Gracie. That's because I was brought up in London and we sound different to the Scots. People that come from different places can have very different accents. Some people have such strong accents that even if they are speaking English, you can't understand them," he laughed.

Gracie smiled too. She liked Sean's accent. "What other kind of accents can you do, Sean?" asked Ava. Sean started speaking in lots of funny voices and had the girls in stitches laughing, trying to copy him, with very little success!

"What is your favourite part of the job?" asked Skye.

"Acting is great fun and I am lucky that I really love my job. However, in order to be able to act, you first have to be offered the work so the best bit of the job is probably the phone-call telling you that you have a job! I really enjoy all aspects of being on set, shooting a scene, meeting the rest of the cast and crew and seeing how scenes come together," he said.

"What is the worst part of the job?" asked Ava.

"I'd say that the unpredictability is the worst aspect. Being an actor is not a stable job for many people. Having said that, I would find a nine to five job boring, but when you are not sure where your next work is coming from, it can be quite daunting! It is certainly not a job for everyone in that respect," he explained.

Sean with his fellow band-mates, acting in *Songs for Amy*.

"How does the film get made?" asked Gracie.

"It depends what kind of film you are making," replied Sean. "In simple terms, you first need to go to the location where the film is being 'shot' or filmed. There you meet the costume designer and make-up artists who decide how you are going to look on 'set', which means how you will end up looking on the screen. Next, you meet the other actors and do a 'read-

Sean filming in Ireland.

through' with them. This is basically a rehearsal, working out how the characters in the film get on with each other and how the script works, with each actor interacting with the other.

During rehearsals, we work out where to stand, where the camera is to be positioned, and so on. Much of this work is done by the film Director who is trying to get the right look for the film, working out the different angles of the shoot.

Once we are all rehearsed and ready, we shoot the film, which just means that the camera starts recording. The time for this varies very much depending on whether it is a low or high budget film, a TV series and so on. It normally takes several months and in some cases, years," he said.

"In between shoots it's a good idea to sit, rest and conserve energy because you can be there from 6am until 10pm, depending on the day, and you have to be equally good at your job from first thing in the morning until last thing at night!" he smiled.

"If there are lots of cameras, how do you know which one to look at?" asked Ava.

"That is a very good question, Ava!" smiled Sean. "The answer is none of them. It is really important that you never look straight at the camera. You have to pretend it's not there at all! If you looked straight at the camera during a film, it would look really weird on the screen when you saw it in the cinema.

You also have to pretend that the crew are not there. That includes the people who are holding the camera, the boom for the sound, the make-up people and so on. There can easily be thirty people around you during filming, so you really have to concentrate not to look at either them or the camera!" he explained.

Duncan, the Director of Photography (or DoP), filming Sean in *Songs for Amy*.

"Are you there all the time?" asked Skye.

"It depends on your role in the film," said Sean. "If you have a small part or a 'cameo' role, you are only there for a short period of time, sometimes only a day. If you have a lead role, you are shooting most days.

The person in charge of the schedule tries to organize the different scenes into a 'shooting schedule', which means that when people come on set, they do all their scenes at once. This helps to reduce costs for travel, as well as save time for costume, wardrobe, etc. If you just shot the scenes as they are laid out in the script, then everyone would be coming and going in a very disorganized fashion!" he said. "Each scene is organised and numbered during filming so that we can go back and find them during the edit."

Sean, Ross and Kevin ready for action.

"What parts do you play?" asked Gracie.

"I play different parts depending on where I am 'cast', which just describes the role they put me in. There are people called 'casting agents' whose job is to find people that suit certain characters. Film-makers use casting agents for most of the bigger jobs as they have a wider network of people that they can access," he explained.

"For example, a casting agent would look at a James Bond film and suggest various different people, contact the film-maker for his feedback and then contact the possible actors to see if they are interested in doing it," he said.

"So what parts have you played?" asked Ava.

"I've played lots of roles as I have been acting since I was very young!" smiled Sean. "My most recent film was *Songs for Amy*, where I played the lead role of Sean O'Malley. I was a musician in the film and I had to learn how to play guitar, which was rather challenging and quite hard work but great fun! I first started acting in Britain when I was five years old, opposite

Sean learning the guitar.

a very famous guy called Laurence Olivier and I've been in lots of different television programs, such as Grange Hill and Eastenders in the UK," explained Sean. "I live in America now and over there I've done various different roles, including films like *Meet the Spartans*," he said.

"How do remember what you have to say in the film?" asked Skye.

"We call them 'lines', which simply means that we have to learn all the words," said Sean. "Everyone has different ways of learning, but for me it is simply repetition! If I can work with someone else, it really helps as it is easier to tell whether I know my lines if I am interacting with another person. After I've learnt the lines, I go on set to see the reaction from the other actors, which can change the way I read mine. It is a very collaborative approach and we all work together to produce the best possible outcome. The actors, writers, directors and all the cast and crew are working together, which is why we are called a 'unit' during filming."

Filming and rehearsing.

"Do you have any tools or equipment that you need for your job?" asked Gracie.

"Each job has different requirements and some need 'props', which are things needed for your role or to get the right background. For example, when I was playing Sean O'Malley in *Songs for Amy*, I was a musician and so I needed a guitar. If I am playing a footballer, I obviously need and football and so on. The most important thing I need to do is research the character I am playing because I need to be as convincing as possible to be credible. I research by reading books and using the computer, as well as speaking to people who understand the character," said Sean.

'Props' include the band van.

"How do you become an actor?" asked Ava.

"There is no clear answer to that question I'm afraid, Ava!" said Sean. "Some people have other jobs that they do for a long time and give it all up to become an actor or actress. Other people decide from a young age that they want to act, so they might go to Drama school for several years to train. Most serious actors get an agent who helps to 'sell' you to film-makers and casting agents. You then need to audition for different parts, or roles, before you can get the work," he explained.

"One of the most important things you can do is educate yourself. If you study really hard at school and continue to educate yourself after school, in as many different things as you can, you are preparing yourself well for acting, as well as any other job. It might sound boring but you cannot underestimate the importance of knowledge as a tool to help you move forward in life! When it comes to acting, the more educated you are about people, their work, the world and so on, the more convincing you can be when you are trying to play someone else," he smiled.

"How do you educate yourself?" asked Skye.

"Well, there are lots of different ways to educate yourself and if you pay attention and keep an open mind in life, you'll be amazed what you can pick up. I go to the library or bookstores a lot and I read as many books as I can," explained Sean. "I also read plays at home and practise the different characters in the play. Some people start with costumes and move onto voice but I always start with trying to find the voice of the character.

I also watch movies that feature good actors so that I can analyse what they are doing, how they react to different situations, and so on. Some people think that actors just turn up and act but the successful actors are very busy researching, reading and always practicing! The more you practise, the better you get. Practicing doesn't have to be boring; it can be great fun too. Do you girls practise to get better at things?" he asked.

Sean practising with his band-mate, Rory.

"Yes," said Ava. "Mama says that you won't be really good at anything unless you work hard and practise. She says some people are naturally better at things than others, but it is often the person who practises and works hard that has the greatest chance of success. She says that applies for most things, including school, work, football or learning an instrument. Do you think that too, Sean?" she asked.

"Absolutely!" he laughed. "There is an old saying that practice makes perfect and you will find that most people who are good at things have put in a huge amount of time and effort to get there! The other thing that is very important is to keep healthy. Anyone that wants to do a professional job needs to be in good health to have the energy to do it properly."

The actors running to chase the getaway van!

"Do you practise doing that thing where the actor pretends to be the person he is playing, even when he is not acting?" asked Gracie.

"You mean 'method acting' I think!" smiled Sean. "That is when someone changes from who they are and pretends to be the person they are in the film. Sometimes these people are 'in character' for a very long time and

 17

they have to completely change their life during that period! I imagine that method acting might be rather inconvenient, not only for the actor, but also for those around him!" he laughed. "No, I don't do method acting, although some people find it works well for them. I tend to method act to a small degree, but not so that it impacts my life and family. For example, if I'm acting in a period drama, or a story from a very long time ago, then I don't really want to be wandering around in a costume from the 1800's all the time!" laughed Sean.

"How do you make money in your work?" asked Ava.

"I am signed up with a theatrical agent who sells me to people that are making TV shows, films or theatre productions. The money I get from each job depends on the budget of the production, as well as my role within it," said Sean.

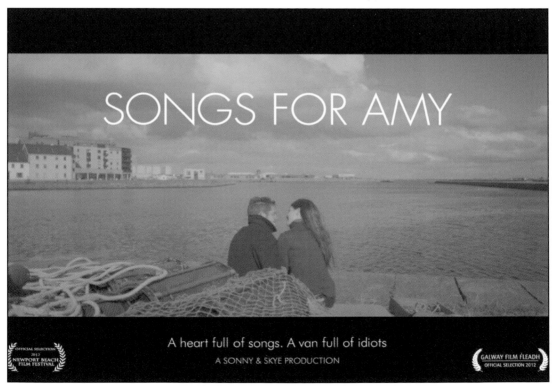

Posters are used to help promote films and TV programmes.

"If it is a big budget film and I play a big part, then I make more money than if it is a small budget film and I play a small part. Just to be confusing, sometimes I play a big part in a small budget film because I like the 'script'. A script is the story that the writer has written, which will be turned into a screenplay for the film," explained Sean.

"When actors finish filming, the job is not yet completed. In order for the film to be sold, there is a huge amount of marketing and publicity that needs to happen to attract people to the cinema to see it. I attend various film festivals and interviews to help promote the film. It is very important to get the promotion of the film right and although it needs to be taken seriously, it can also be really fun," said Sean.

Interviews in America.

Actors Sean, Lorna and Kevin at a festival.

"What do you do if people recognize you in the street?" asked Ava.

"Everyone handles being recognised differently," said Sean. "If someone comes up to me and asks for a photo or an autograph, then I personally find it easier just to say 'yes' and they go off happy. Sometimes, if I am having a private time with my family, I'll maybe ask if I can do it later but I try to say 'yes' if I can. If I say 'no' then they might be disappointed and it is better to think that you have made someone happy if you can, isn't it?" he smiled.

"Yes," replied Gracie. "We are happy and we like to see everyone happy!"

"Exactly" laughed Sean. "If we could make everyone happy, the world would be a better place, so it is important that we do what we can to help others. Even small things can sometimes make a big difference," he smiled.

Sean at an American festival.

Sean with mother and auntie Yaya in Badaneel.

"Do people treat you differently because you are famous?" asked Skye.

"Yes, sometimes. For example, strangers will come and speak to me, which wouldn't happen if I wasn't in films. I am very lucky because I still have lots of my friends from childhood as well as a great family. I try to keep my friends and family close to me as they keep me grounded and I can trust them. Your real friends are friends with you whether you are successful or not. They like you because of who you are, not what you do.

It is important not to get caught up in all the attention because at the end of the day, it's just a job," he said.

Suddenly there was a voice signalling for the film to begin.

"I need to go now girls but it has been really good to meet you and I'm sure we will catch up again one day to see how your investigation into grown-up jobs is going! All the best!"

And with that he waved goodbye and headed into the crowd, chatting to the people around him. The Mackenzie girls thought he was a lovely man and had thoroughly enjoyed their chat about the film world. "I like Sean," said Ava. The other Mackenzie girls nodded. "Me too," they said.

It was very busy in the Badaneel café and Mother appeared with some juice and crisps. They chatted together about what Sean had said and Ava remarked that she liked the idea of being on television and going to parties to promote films.

"Being an actor is a great job, Ava," said Mother, "but it is most certainly not all about parties! When Sean is at events to help promote the film, he is working. He travels a great deal, which can be rather exhausting. Acting has many good sides to it but, like any job, there are also downsides. It is difficult to get consistent work and, if you do become really famous, then there is very little privacy. Famous actors are constantly being bothered by the press, and anyone else who sees them. As with every job, you need to understand the good sides as well as the bad. Only then can you make a decision about what you might do when you grow up," she said.

"Well, it's been a very busy day and I think it's time for these little girls to get to bed," she smiled, as she gathered them together and headed back to the peace and quiet of the house.

It had been another very interesting day and the girls wondered who they would meet next...

The end.

 21

What do the grown-ups do?

The books are available in paperback and e-book and can be purchased through all major bookstores as well as on online. For more information, please check the website

www.kidseducationalbooks.com.

The What do the grown-ups do? series in order of publishing:

Book 1: Joe the fisherman

Book 2: Papa the stockfarmer

Book 3: Sean the actor

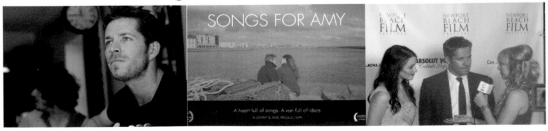

Book 4: Fiona the doctor

Book 5: Richard the vet

Book 6: Gordon the wildlife filmmaker

What do the grown-ups do? series

The What do the grown-ups do? series is based on life in the northwest Highlands of Scotland, in a village called Badaneel, and follows three little local girls as they investigate the world of 'grown-up' jobs. Designed for children aged five to ten years, the aim is to educate them about working life, and the world around them, in a light-hearted manner.

Sean visits Badaneel for the screening of his latest film. Before he heads off to meet the guests, he spends some time with the Mackenzie girls, educating them on the pros and cons of acting. He has them in stitches with different accents, talks about the enjoyable, yet unpredictable nature of acting life and explains why you must never look at the camera!

"May all of children's non-fiction literature begin to engage students as McLellan's books do. If this is a new trend in children's books, teachers across the US would be so grateful."
Marlene Moyer, 5th & 6th Grade teacher, Nevada, USA.

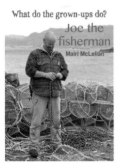

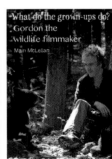